This special signed edition
is limited to 1000 numbered copies.

This is copy 933.

SILVIA MORENO-GARCIA

The RETURN *of the* SORCERESS

The RETURN *of the* SORCERESS

Silvia Moreno-Garcia

SUBTERRANEAN PRESS 2021

The Return of the Sorceress

Edited by Yanni Kuznia

First Edition

ISBN

978-1-64524-030-3

Subterranean Press

PO Box 190106

Burton, MI 48519

subterraneanpress.com

Manufactured in the United States of America

THE YELLOW HOUSE

ONLY THE MOON spied on the woman from behind a cloud as she stumbled across the narrow and twisted alleyways, one hand brushing against a wall, trying to remain upright. Her other hand was pressed against her side, blood seeping from the wound, blood on her fingertips.

In the dark the buildings had no color. The yellow house, three stories high, was rendered very much like any other house. All of these buildings could have been the abode where she first lodged when she arrived in this neighbourhood, seventeen and as bright as a newly-minted coin. She'd been a callow girl from the provinces, gone to the city to seek her fortune with the heedless optimism of youth. Now she crawled back to her beginnings, dirt and muck clinging to her clothes, her bones paining her.

She'd been wandering in the alleys, in the dark, for what seemed a small eternity and she feared that she'd never find it, that the house was an illusion that she'd fabricated. But she tightened the clumsy bandage she'd tied and kept pressing against the wound, shuffling on.

I refuse to die, she thought and though her body screeched and begged for her to give in, she would not let it, ordering a foot to slide forward, ordering a hand to cling to a wall. The high forms of sorcery all require tools and careful processes. Glyphs, knives, words. At its most rudimentary form, however, magic is willpower and though she no longer had much magic left, inside of her there was still her colossal willpower.

This itself was a form of sorcery, survival singing through her nerves and forcing tendons to bend, flesh to press forward, tired bones be damned.

At last the moon unveiled itself and its light drifted down, illuminating the street and allowing the woman to catch a glimpse of the faded yellow paint and the familiar shutters. She walked up the three steps to the back door and took a breath, feeling beneath the wood, touching the warding spells she'd cast upon this place. Nothing terribly fancy, mostly a sense of malaise that would drive thieves away and a poison spell or two, just in case. Besides, the house was in a rundown quarter of little importance and it was crawling with rats—such vermin was not native to the city, but it had adapted well enough to the canals—and had nothing worth stealing. At least, nothing most people would think worth stealing.

She unlocked the door, tracing an old sigil in the air, and walked in, going up to the third floor. Though she had bought the yellow house, she did not visit it. Why would she? The yellow house had been part of a previous life.

She found her old room, bare now, covered with dust and quiet. It had never been this quiet. Ten students had lodged in this house, all under the tutelage of a minor sorcerer. One of these students had been Xellah, handsome and astute and only six months older than her. It was Xellah, imbued with the bravado of youth, who had suggested that they attempt to find themselves a better Master, for if they were to be apprentices shouldn't they aim for the best? Should they not look towards the grand pyramid at the center of the city? Should they not seek to learn under the Master of the House of Sorcery, under Teotah, owner of the Diamond Heart?

He'd said it half in jest but Yalxi had latched onto the idea with all seriousness and when he hesitated, it was she who ultimately pulled him forward: Xellah was always one for grandiose plans and few results. Yet that time, dragged by the force of her willpower, they accomplished that dream they'd first spun one lazy afternoon. They had been accepted as apprentices to that sorcerer of sorcerers, Master Teotah. And in time the young apprentice, the hardy girl from the provinces with the quick and ferocious mind, had become Mistress Yalxi. Decked in jewels, swathed in silks, sitting atop the pyramid. Mistress Yalxi.

Now Yalxi had a gash on her head, a wound on her belly and a foot that throbbed. She was covered in sweat and filth, stinking of her own piss. So much for her grandiose plans and dreams.

Her palm slid against the wall and she winced. One, two, three paces and then she pulled at a stone and revealed a tiny, hollowed out space and inside of it a piece of cloth. She unwrapped the cloth and beheld the ring.

It was silver, with a modest pearl, and felt cold against her skin. She detected nothing, not the slightest intimation of life. Perhaps it was gone, the spirit had departed. It could have seeped into the stone and trickled down into the canal and again into the world.

If this was so, then she was truly finished.

She placed the ring on her index finger. "It is I, Yalxi," she told the ring.

Under the skittish light of the moon the ring remained cold and ordinary, nothing but metal and the diminutive pearl. She licked her lips and held out her hand. "Awake," she ordered.

She felt it then, it was the slightest twitch and a voice replied in a whisper as soft as the wing of a moth. "Yalxi, I remember you. I remember all for you."

"Yes, it's me."

"It has been a long time. How many years?"

"Ten and more."

Nahuales often manifested in animal shapes, rarely they adopted human visages and these were often monstrous. Some could show themselves as forces of nature, like a bolt of lightning or an icy wind. This nahual, however, remained stubbornly inside the ring, curled tight, perhaps as a show of its displeasure. Or because it did not have the strength to attempt more.

They were, the both of them, rather diminished.

"You're dying."

"I'm wounded," she corrected. "Grievously wounded, but not dead yet."

"Presently, though."

"Not if you assist me."

"Why should I?"

"Because I've returned. And because I offer salt and blood."

"Where is your precious Diamond Heart, Yalxi? And he? Your most beloved? Where is Xellah?"

"Salt and blood, I said."

She felt the nahual smirk. "If I let you die in this chamber I'll get my blood and then I'll find myself a foolish youth with a hankering of magic to feed me their tears."

"They will not be me."

"I don't like *you* right this instant. Maybe I did, but not now."

"But you like my strength and you like my anger. You always did. And I still have that," she said and made a fist, because if there was something that she could give now it was pure fury. Xellah would die by her hand and she would recoup the diamond, even if she had to raze that pyramid brick by brick.

"I liked your passion, Yalxi. Dearest, dearest Yalxi."

"So, then? Will you help me?"

The nahual chuckled, derisive, but she felt as if something unfurled, like a cat stretching its limbs. She dragged a finger down her cheek, down the trail of her tears and then she untied the bandage, letting the blood flow, letting it stain her fingers.

"Salt and blood for you," she said, kneeling and held her hand out.

She felt a prick on her finger and a tiny tug as the nahual bit into her hand.

"My lady," the nahual whispered.

She bowed her head and closed her eyes, for she was tired. She dreamt. Terrible, wild images of water and darkness and death and there was a rotten taste in her mouth.

THE ORANGE GARDEN

SHE WOKE TO the scent of orange blossoms, in a narrow bed, the covers up to her chin. She slid a hand against her torso and touched the bandage underneath. Her bones felt as brittle as threads of silk, her head throbbed and the bad taste in her mouth had not abated. She had retched while she slept but the nahual or someone else had not allowed her to choke on her own vomit. Small mercy, that was. She would not die in such an undignified manner.

She refused to die at all. Not now. She stared at the ceiling and took a deep breath.

Yalxi sat up. She was no longer in the yellow house. Her room was small and furnished in a simple, spare fashion. The nahual, now turned into a white pigeon, sat on the window sill, smoothing its feathers with its beak.

Had the nahual really done her bidding? Brought her where it must? The door opened and in walked a woman in a purple habit, carrying a tray. Axahuite, rendered older, her mouth now bracketed with two lines. Her dark eyes swept over her, unimpressed, and she placed the tray on Yalxi's lap.

Despite the woman's grim expression Yalxi allowed herself to smile because, yes, the nahual had looked into her heart and obeyed her wishes. She'd escaped and she was safe. At least, for now.

"You're awake. That is good. It means you're not as mangled as I thought," Axahuite said.

"That's a matter of opinion," Yalxi replied, rubbing her wrists, feeling the scabs under her fingertips.

The food was simple fare. Water, bread, an orange cut in two, beans and rice. She did not wait for permission to eat, quickly stuffing a bit of bread into her mouth. Her meals had been inconsistent while she languished in the cells. Besides, she'd always taken what she could and been quick at it. Long before the city, long before the yellow house, the provinces had offered meager opportunities and even meager meals. She'd travelled with a group of itinerant sorcerers, apprentices only in the most crude sense of the word. They'd fought like wild dogs for bread crusts and a thin cut of meat.

"My heartfelt thanks for this," Yalxi said, as she shoved a spoonful of food into her mouth, not wishing to entirely forget her manners.

"It's not as if I had much of a choice. Your nahual was insistent that you needed my assistance."

"I very much do. As you can see, I lack a certain diamond."

"Then it is true and Xellah is now Master of the Guild," Axahuite said, sounding thoughtful.

"News must travel slow. I've been imprisoned for weeks."

"We do not concern ourselves with much of what happens outside these walls. The scuffles of the guild members are of little importance to us."

Axahuite stared at her while Yalxi ate until Yalxi tipped her chin up and stared back at the woman. Axahuite knitted her hands together.

"I thought he would have killed you."

"Then he wouldn't have been able to bleed me."

She didn't know if her apprentices had been as lucky. Xellah might have killed them all. They could be imprisoned, as she had been. Or else they'd sworn their allegiances to their new master. The later would not have been unusual. In fact, it would be expected. Sorcery was an exhausting, dangerous game. When she'd been young, it had seemed simpler. But the magic had worn down her bones through the years and without the diamond she felt almost unable to lift a finger.

Yet now she had the ring with the pearl and an idea.

When Yalxi finished her meal, Axahuite took away the tray and undid her bandages, carefully looking at the wound, before applying an ointment and changing the wrappings.

"It's healing at a decent pace."

"That's good news at last."

"For the both of us," Axahuite said. "You can't remain here. Xellah will come looking for you."

"It may take him a day or two."

"I won't allow you to endanger us. You should leave tonight."

"He has the diamond heart."

Axahuite said nothing. The purple folds of her habit suited her much better than the white garments of the novice and her face, grown sterner, was also more appropriate.

"I must have it back," Yalxi said.

"That is your business and none of mine. Be gone by nightfall. The games sorcerers play never concerned me," the woman said and she made a motion, as if to leave the room.

"They concerned Itzyul."

Axahuite stood still. The white curtains fluttered, a gentle breeze toying with them.

"The diamond heart will have made Xellah terribly powerful and very dangerous. Our master's essence still clings to the jewel and those who are weak-willed will succumb to his voice. Xellah will become more and more like Master Teotah. He's not as strong as I am. I reigned over the jewel but Xellah will be ruled by the diamond. What will you do when Xellah marches, hungry for blood, through the city? Hungry for people like Itzyul. I must have the jewel back."

"To save us all from certain doom?" Axahuite said, chuckling. "How selfless of you."

"I'm saying what must be done."

"You're saying what you must do in order to regain your seat at the guild. Don't attempt to mask it with lies. Your ambition is naked and raw, it always was. But one selfish sorcerer is as bad as the next."

There was some truth to that, but Yalxi shook her head. "He'll be worse. He'll be exactly like Teotah."

"And I suppose you've been the very soul of kindness?"

"I thought you didn't indulge in idle gossip behind these walls," Yalxi said sweetly.

On the window sill the pigeon cocked its head and looked at the women with its black little eyes, stifling its laughter. Itzyul had loved birds, had kept doves. Yalxi wondered if the nahual was mocking her with this shape. Perhaps it was a mere coincidence.

"You're strong enough for jokes, then you're strong enough to leave."

Yalxi held up her palm in the air. "Cast me out if you wish, but I am no liar. I never was. Xellah will bring pain and suffering to the city, and when he does, you must remember you could have stopped it."

"Did you tell *her* the same thing, when you convinced her to murder your old master?"

"I didn't have to convince your sister of anything. She knew the truth, just as you know it now. She did what was right."

"She was a fool," Axahuite said, but softly.

Yalxi had not thought about her friend in many years, but now she clearly remembered the girl's voice, her irrepressible laughter. She'd been a bright creature, eager to learn. The memory of her death, clear as glass, swept through her and the sight of her mangled corpse lingered in Yalxi's eyes. It was vivid, she could have almost touched the dead girl's face.

It was the nahual's doing. He'd unfurled the memory for her, pulled it out for her to see. A cruel gesture and she could almost hear a snicker as she turned her head and pressed a hand against her mouth, feeling sick.

Stop it, she thought, glaring at the pigeon.

"Are you unwell?" Axahuite asked, concerned. The abrasive, defensive mask she'd worn was crumbling.

"Just a dizzy spell," she lied.

Axahuite nodded, her hands hidden in the folds of her robe. Her face was serious, but softer. "You really think he'd be as dangerous as your old master?"

"Yes. As long as he has the diamond heart his magic is not only magnified, but he commands the Sorcerers' Guild and the magic of his apprentices, making him terribly powerful."

"If that's the case, how do you expect to defeat him?"

"I'll need the diamond fragment Itzyul was buried with."

"You want to open her coffin? How dare you."

Axahuite's face was once again hard and Yalxi knew she risked being dragged out into the street, but she pressed on.

"I must find our old master's bones. We erased the memory of the journey, but the diamond would remember. It contains a fragment of our master's essence and will seek to be reunited with the rest. It's compelled to do so."

"And what will you do if it does lead you back to your master's gravesite? What if somehow you regain the diamond heart? You'll sit atop that pyramid again and the city will bleed, one way or another. Your spells are made with pain and you cut down your enemies like others cut wheat."

Some enemies deserve to be cut, she thought. Besides, she was a guild master, not some carnival magician. This was the game of power which each sorcerer must play.

"And he'll be worse."

"Yes. Worse. A tyrant. A monster. Once you said you'd destroy the jewel, but look at what you did," the woman said, chuckling. "You crawled upon the throne, your way paved in blood, and that diamond clutched against your bosom. You broke your word."

"I'll destroy the Diamond Heart. I'll do it, this time around. I'll swear it in blood, if you want. On her grave."

Her vehemence seemed to surprise them both and they stared at each other.

"I must think about it," Axahuite said and hastily left the room.

Yalxi took a deep breath and moved to stand before the window, looking at the large, inner courtyard beneath. There were many orange trees and the air was scented with the sweetness of their blossoms. At the other end of the courtyard was a small stone temple dedicated to the virgin moon goddess and beneath the temple the crypts where the acolytes of her order were buried.

Itzyul had been interred there, after a dispensation from the order, for her sister did not want to be far from her. She must be only bones now. As must their old master.

The diamond.

She must have it back.

Spellcasting aged you on the inside. She was thirty-six but felt a woman of sixty without the magic jewel. Magic was a game for the young and yet it was experience that honed the magic. This paradox meant every sorcerer clung to whatever tricks they had. Blood, from every possible source to make spells more potent. And nahuales. The diamond had provided her with much strength, erased the damage to her organs. Like this she was fallible and the nahual in the pearl ring not nearly enough.

"You lie prettily, telling her that you'll destroy the diamond," the dove said.

"Perhaps I mean it."

"I know you better than yourself. *Perhaps* guilt overwhelmed you for a second but it won't last."

"She did not die by my hand so there's no guilt to be had."

"Precious girl, do you forget? Yes, you do. But I don't. If you wish to remember, I'll assist you."

"I don't need your assistance with that," she muttered, and the bird laughed. But her dreams were awful, filled with blood and the smothering embrace of water. Filled with Itzyul's tears, too. In the end she shoved the covers away and stared at the ceiling, her brow slick with sweat, her head throbbing again.

And the nahual was right because she couldn't quite remember but now that the ring of pearl was on her finger she couldn't forget either, caught in a liminal point between shadows. Caught and dashed against the fury of the past and the devastating, bitter present.

The scent of orange blossoms was stronger in the morning, as if new flowers had opened to greet her. She undid the bandage and examined the wound, which looked pink and raw. But it was healing with astonishing quickness, courtesy of both the nahual's magic and the care she'd received. A novice had brought more food and water, and Yalxi ate and waited, feeding the bird a few drops of blood from her index finger. It lapped them up greedily.

They had left for her a change of clothes. It was not the white habit of the novices, but a coarse shirt and a skirt, the kind they gave to the poor when the members of the order engaged in their charitable deeds. The clothes chaffed against her skin and the shoes were of tough, cheap leather that made her long for her silks and sandals. After she finished dressing she plaited her hair. One long, black braid that reached the waist.

She hesitated, her fingers stilling, as she remembered plaiting Itzyul's hair in better days, when they had both been eager apprentices, the sides of their head shorn. They had known then, even in the naivety of youth, the might and power, and also the infamy of their master. But emboldened with the bravado of their few years they had not thought harm would come to them. And back in the beginning, Master Teotah had been different. Less callous. Less cruel.

"But cold, then, even then," the nahual said, reading her thoughts. "Nor burning. Burning like the ember you are."

"Shush," she said, but she allowed it to drink from her blood again. Only the tip of the finger and not the armpit. She had no strength for more. But the nahual was pleased and it curled up, in the shape of a cat, next to her head, purring.

She napped a little and then woke, startled, and slept again. It was like bobbing up and down an ocean. The aches of her wounded body delivered her back to consciousness, but so did treacherous memories, unpleasant dreams. Yet she squeezed some rest from those restless hours.

Axahuite returned late in the afternoon, as she had hoped she would. "Let us do this quick. There is a rumor that men from the Sorcerers' Guild are about with their hounds," she said.

That she had not hoped for, but it couldn't be helped.

Yalxi followed her outside and across the courtyard. By the entrance of the little stone temple waited three novices dressed in their white habits. When they saw Axahuite they bowed their heads, lit their lanterns and opened the doors for them.

The city had been built, partially, atop marshes, but the patch of land upon which Axahuite's order rested was solid ground. Therefore, underneath the temple, the nuns of the order had carved tunnels and crypts where the bodies of the dead rested. Yalxi had not returned here in over a decade. Now she watched as the novices pulled a sarcophagus from its ledge and pried it open.

Axahuite held a little leather bag filled with herbs, which dangled from a cord around her neck, and pressed it against her nose, warding off the scent of mold and rat's droppings. Yalxi had no such remedy, so she simply stared as the women worked.

The body was wrapped in purple cloth and the novices untied several knots until a skeleton lay bare under the yellowish light of the lanterns. The dead woman clasped a small filigree silver box between her hands.

Although Axahuite turned her head during the unwrapping, Yalxi did not flinch. It seemed to her that the Itzyul she'd known and the corpse on display were two entirely different entities. Therefore she had no qualms reaching forward and grabbing the box, carefully opening it.

There, upon purple velvet cloth, lay a minuscule diamond shard. They'd left it as a one might leave a medal upon a soldier's tomb. It had been such an insignificant bit of the jewel that Yalxi did not mind parting with it. Nor had she imagined she might have use for it. Only after she had been betrayed and imprisoned had the thought occurred to her that she might need it.

"Reverend Mother," a novice said, rushing into the chamber, flustered, "there are men coming. Men in yellow, from the Sorcerers' Guild."

"I must go," Yalxi said.

"But go where in your state?" Axahuite asked. "We might be able to hide you."

"No, you were right. I pose a danger to you and should leave. I'll need the purse around your neck," she said pointing at one of the novices.

"What for?" the novice asked.

"Do as she says," Axahuite ordered.

The novice quickly handed it over. Yalxi stuffed the silver box inside and placed the cord around her neck.

Axahuite gave Yalxi a few coins and she also stuffed them inside the purse.

"I'll make a contribution to your order when I return," she promised.

"Keep your word about the diamond. Burn it to ashes. That's all I ask."

Yalxi nodded and snatched a lantern from one of the novices, hurrying up the stairs. It was not yet dusk and for a moment she allowed herself to look up and contemplate the sky, catching her breath.

"Are you sure this is a good idea? We could hide, as she said," the nahual, shaped like a white cat, told her.

"No. If he's looking for me in this area of the city it's because he suspects what I'm doing. Or someone opened their mouth."

"Or the hounds have your scent."

"I doubt that."

"If they do, you won't be able to hide."

"We'll see."

She crossed the courtyard and went back into the living quarters of the novices. She found a side door that led onto the street and slipped outside.

"Where are we headed?"

"The Court of Thieves," she said, moving aside for three water carriers who walked with the huge ceramic jugs of water strapped to thcir backs, heading back and forth from the fountain that supplied the houses that lacked their own private water source with fresh drinking water.

The nahual, still in the shape of a cat, walked quickly next to her. "What do you expect to do there?"

"Buy my way out of the city. If Xellah has hounds and sorcerers after me, he will no doubt be watching each and every one of the great bridges."

"If that is the case, then you'll never get out."

"Not without the help of the Guild of Thieves."

They crossed three little bridges and the narrow streets quickly widened. They were headed in the direction of the White Plaza, which was bordered by one of the seven great canals. This was the most expedient way towards their final destination. Across the White Plaza and then further east until they reached the Guild of Thieves. But as they crossed a fourth bridge, the nahual stopped and hissed, its ears flat against its skull.

"What?" she asked.

"Hounds."

They were still far from the sunken palace that served as the seat of the Guild of Thieves. Left and right there rose squat buildings with lines of washing upon the roofs and nearby there wafted the stench of the fishmongers stalls. They were close to a market.

"Come," she said and picked up the pace, walking as fast as she could, despite the pain on her side. She had not fully healed and each quick step pulled at the raw flesh.

But she could hear them now, the black hounds barking in the streets and other dogs—inside houses, inside businesses—barking back in fear. The black hounds with their jaws like iron.

"You cannot outrun them," the nahual said.

"We'll see," she said as they emerged onto the plaza where the fishmongers set their stalls. It was one of the large markets, where merchants sold their wares every day rather than the little ones where the trade was conducted twice a week. There were fresh sharks and rays, and also salted fish, large and tiny ones. It was late in the day and soon they would begin to light their lamps. Trade was brisk here in the summer, even late in the evening.

The dogs howled. They would be there any minute now.

"What are we doing here? We should be running."

"There," she muttered when she spotted an old beggar in a filthy gray cape wandering around the stalls, muttering about alms. She tapped him on the shoulder and he turned around, looking at her with bloodshot eyes.

"Alms for the poor, miss?" he asked.

"How about a trade," she said.

"What could I trade you?"

"Your cloak," she said and produced a coin.

The beggar licked his lips. "Two would be more like it."

From the corner of her eye she could see men in yellow cloaks and yellow leather gloves, huge black dogs walking by their side, growling. The crowds parted for them, housewives and servants and peddlers making way for the sorcerers.

"Two, then."

He handed her the cloak and she wrapped it around her shoulders. A young boy was dragging a bucket filled with fish guts down an alleyway. He likely intended to toss it into a canal.

She followed the child, gritting her teeth through the pain as she shuffled her feet quick as she could. She couldn't run. They'd notice, but also she simply wasn't physically able to attempt it. Not with pain radiating down her right side, her muscles on fire.

"Boy," she said.

The child looked up at her, curious, holding the handle of the bucket with two hands.

"I'll trade you for that bucket," she said and pulled one of the coins in her pouch.

The child looked at her with interest and nodded, his palm outstretched. She handed him the coin and picked the bucket. The child ran back the way he'd come. She leaned against the wall and took a breath before sinking her hand into the mess of fish guts and slapping it on her face. She rubbed fish guts on her cloak, which already smelled of vomit and was crusted with grime.

When she was done she shuffled towards the end of the street to the canal. There were two posts there, to tie boats, and steps leading down into the water. But there were no barges.

She tossed the bucket into the water and sat next to one of the posts, half-hidden by shadows. The nahual was still a cat and it looked at her curiously. She could hear the murmur of the water licking at her feet and the panting of the dogs nearby. Closer now, oh too close.

She bit her hand until it hurt, the pain so sharp she could think of nothing else. Just the pain and the stench in her nose. Fish guts and sweat and garbage, and her mind was a searing blank. And she squeezed her eyes shut until tears ran down her cheeks, savaging her own flesh.

She opened her eyes again and stared at the canal. The roar of the hounds was gone, they had moved away. She let her hand fall against her side and chuckled when the cat came over, to lick at her wounds, tasting her blood.

"Don't let a drop go to waste, right?" she muttered.

"I've starved."

"So have I," she said and shoved the cat off.

She spit into the canal.

THE BLUE PALACE

The Thieves Quarter announced itself long before you reached it by the shadows of its tall, tottering tenements. Thick as weeds they rose on each side of the canals, built on soil that was too soft, too marshy, and that had been haphazardly dried out. The fountains here were broken or spit out a green muck and the statues lining the boulevards held up mutilated arms.

Now that night had fallen the windows of the drinking dens and whorehouses glowed with a spectral light, illuminating her path. The glass on many windows was blue or a pale green, coloring the night accordingly.

She walked slowly but with purpose and dressed in such poor clothes, her head bowed, that the denizens of the alleys did not bother her, thinking her one of their own. The nahual had turned into a skinny white dog and followed her, merry and eager.

She had not been back here in many years either. When she'd been young, when she had lived in that yellow house and was only a skinny apprentice of no importance, they'd come to buy ingredients. You could purchase teeth and hair and sometimes the corpse of a dead man. Down, closer to the Third Canal, there were also merchants of salts and various dyes who sold their wares cheaper than others in the city. This was also the place where young students might avail themselves to the most affordable drinks.

She had been studious and not one for the drinking dens with their fermented agave, nor the taverns with their wines and spirits. But Xellah liked to be merry, he liked to be careless, he liked the thrill of the night. His wildness contrasted with her primness—she was a country girl, modest and a little rough. He was the byblow of some lord, tutored but penniless. Their odd alchemy somehow produced a balanced whole.

She rubbed a hand roughly against her mouth as they emerged onto a large plaza and she saw the decrepit palace that was the Court of Thieves. It was gently sinking, one side of it dragged down into the too-soft ground. It was a lopsided, beautiful monstrosity decorated with blue and white tiles, all of them featuring delicate sea anemones and corals and playful fish.

It should have never been built on that location. But the conquerors who had remade the city had dragged many canals that should not have been dragged, placed stones where they should not have been placed and centuries later—after endless wars and games of power, the taking and retaking of bits of the city—this was the result. A blue tile palace that little by little was being dragged down to its doom.

She looked at the long windows and the five large arches running along the portico, trying to spot sorcerers in yellow cloaks who might be waiting in ambush, but saw none. Her hasty disguise must be holding true. They had not picked her scent.

"Or else they're in the shadows," the dog said.

"Only one way to find out."

The dog glanced at her worriedly but followed along.

There were no guards barring the doors. The Court of Thieves, unlike the Court of Sorcerers and the Court of Assassins, was open to all. In hallways and staircases and alcoves there congregated the riffraff of this quarter. Rough-looking women with knives at their waist standing under the dim light of a rusty chandelier and men in rags playing dice in rooms hung with precious tapestries that were being systematically devoured by eager moths. They sold, bartered, killed and slept here, in this damp palace with mold on the walls.

She walked past them, walked into the great hall with its enormous torches and finally beheld the throne. It was a huge carved and gilded chair which had once belonged to the rightful owners of this palace and who were now rightfully dead—of the original five guilds, they were now reduced to three and this had been the seat of power of one of those previous guilds.

In the chair, carved with images of sea life, of fish and sirens and dolphins, sat a woman, her hair gray, carelessly observing the people around her, the loathsome band of thieves and beggars who served as her courtiers. The chamber was thick with noise, with inebriated conversations, and from the ceiling there hung a golden censer, steadily burning a sticky, black substance which could never clear the miasma reigning in this room.

The woman on the throne was drinking from a large cup encrusted with gem stones and smiling. Her single, left eye smiled too, black and alert. Her neck was wrapped thick with chains of silver and gold and she wore a ring on each finger. But these were not magical devices, no spirits resided in the gemstones. It was common plunder.

As Yalxi dragged her feet along the long, red carpet leading to the throne she finally found an obstacle. A huge woman, her thick arms bulging with muscle, stepped forward and shook her head.

"What business do you have here?"

"I seek an audience."

"You've got the wrong day of the week, then. Come back the day after tomorrow."

"I can't wait until tomorrow," she said and took a step, but the woman yanked her by the arm.

The dog growled and Yalxi, too tired to pretend courtesy, sank her nails into the woman's wrist and hissed a crude spell. The strong woman yelped, raising her hands as if she'd been burnt, then narrowed her eyes at Yalxi. Two other women, equally strong, were now very interested in her and fingering their daggers.

"Sorcerous scum," the woman said, but before she could throw a punch Yalxi yanked her hood back and revealed her face, staring at the Mistress of the Guild of Thieves.

"Stop," the one-eyed woman said and held her hand in the air. "Come here."

She walked up to the throne and the queen looked down at her, grinning. "Why it *is* Grand Mistress Yalxi, smelling like she was dragged through a pile of garbage, no less. For a moment I believed I was hallucinating. I thought you were dead."

"I keep hearing that."

"What are you doing here?"

"I'll tell you if you grant me a private audience, for it's not news that ought to be shared."

The woman crooked a finger at her, grinning. "Come."

They ventured to an alcove directly behind the audience room, a small and somewhat cozy space decorated with silks and velvets and more of those great censers to keep the whiff of rot at bay. The Mistress of the Guild of Thieves refilled her cup of wine while three armed guards watched Yalxi, their hands at the ready. In a corner, atop a pile of crimson cushions, sat a man playing a six-string lute. In another corner there was a collection of various silver dishes, piled with food. Thick, dark grapes and pale fish and even roast pheasant. The white dog sniffed at the food.

“Your friends are paranoid,” Yalxi said, glancing at the woman who had grabbed her by the arm. “I’m not about to spill blood in your court and break every rule and vow we hold holy.”

“Just last week two of my favorites were fished from the canals, their faces bloated and black, and their bodies drained of blood. Sorcerers are leeches, so you might have to pardon the ‘paranoid’ attitude we have.”

“Xellah’s handiwork? He moves against you?” Yalxi asked innocently, though she could guess the answer.

“Not quite.”

“Not *yet*. Do you mind? I’m a little thirsty,” she said, pointing at the goblet and wine decanter set atop the table.

The one-eyed woman filled a second cup with wine and handed it to Yalxi, frowning. “What do you know about Xellah’s plans?”

“Nothing, but I know Xellah and he’s a greedy, hungry creature. He’ll never settle for less when he can have more. If he’s begun to move against you, he will not cease until every tile in this palace has been cracked and tossed into the canals.”

The woman sat on a divan while Yalxi sipped her wine. She tapped her very long, crimson nails against her thigh, the rings flashing under the blue light spilling from the glass lamps which, like the censer, dangled from golden chains from the ceiling. Yalxi might have been impressed with such displays, once upon a time, when she was a mere girl new to the city. Now this struck her as tacky. But she had need of the Guild of Thieves.

"You still haven't explained why you are here, Mistress Yalxi. Is it to spin tall tales for me?"

"You think that a tall tale? I call it logic."

"Xellah would never do battle against us."

"And yet you are, as you just admitted, a little paranoid. Why?"

"Small quarrels take place now and then. Anyway, I'm more interested in your tale. What exactly happened between you and Xellah?"

He betrayed me and I shall flay him once I get my diamond back, she thought.

The dog had found a bone and was toying with it. Yalxi sat down on the floor and scratched its ear. "A small quarrel," she said simply. "He'll do much worse to you."

The one-eyed woman smiled, showing off two golden teeth. "Perhaps if Xellah were to receive word that you are here he might forget the small quarrel he has with me."

"I don't think so. I've come to save your life."

"*My* life. You come here, looking like you haven't eaten in three months and you are going to save *me?*"

The woman laughed. Her guards seemed amused too. In the corner the man with the lute played his song, seemingly unconcerned with their conversation.

"Yes, your life," Yalxi continued. "Because Xellah did not overthrow me just so he could be idle and content. Ambition gnaws at his gut. Why should he have to stomach two other guilds when there could be but one? Why can't he crown himself a Warlock Emperor and rule over all?"

"Because he'd never have the chance. The other atlepetls would not allow it. Xellah may be foolish enough to take on one guild, but he would not take on two. Even if he could, he would never triumph against the other cities, with their own guilds. You are not the only sorcerers on the face of the earth."

"Once, a long time ago, my old Master thought it was possible. Teotah, who took your eye. Teotah who has returned. Perhaps he'll take your tongue, this time."

That single name did the trick. The one-eyed woman's face turned scarlet with rage.

"Go, out, all of you," the Mistress said raising her hand and pointing at the door. The guards seemed surprised, but they did not protest. The man with the lute took his instrument and hastily departed.

The white dog, still gnawing at the bone, raised its head and looked at the women.

"My tongue, you say? You should watch yours."

"I speak no lies," Yalxi said simply.

"You've sat atop that pyramid for fifteen years, you've worn that diamond pectoral for all to see. Teotah is dead and we both know it."

"Teotah is dead and gone, and yet not. His spirit lingers inside the diamond and it has infected Xellah. Practice your curtsies: the sorcerer returns."

The one-eyed woman shrugged. "Well, what of it? Your old master annihilated two guilds, but it benefited us in the end."

"And your eye. Was that also for your benefit?"

The older woman stood up and glared down at Yalxi. She was still tall, still strong. Even if her hair had gone gray and her hands were molted with age, Yalxi did not doubt she was still quick with a knife.

"What do you and your mangy cur want, Yalxi?" she asked, her voice sharp.

"I must leave the city and Xellah will be watching the three causeways and the great canals."

"You intend me to spirit you out, then, and in the process I'll earn Xellah's enmity. All because of some imaginary doom that may never come to pass."

"My point is you've already earned his enmity."

"Not if I tie you down right now and drag your bony body to that pyramid of yours."

"Do this and you'll destroy the only weapon that might save you."

There was a long silence. The one-eyed woman, the Queen of Thieves who ruled over cutthroats and liars and cheats, who feared neither princes nor criminals, and who had sent many an unsuspecting fool to the grave, had grown weary.

THE SINKING PALACE was not to Yalxi's liking. It was too crammed with both furniture and people, it felt unclean even when she was shown to a room that was well maintained, its velvet curtains intact, the beautiful gilded mirror adorning one wall cloudy but still glimmering.

It was not the pyramid and her neck was bare, that was the problem.

She missed the Diamond Heart and longed for its power. She hungered for her home more than she did for food or drink, even if she plucked a handful of grapes and tossed them in her mouth.

Two servants filled a tub with water and Yalxi undressed, sinking into its warmth and groaning at the feeling of the salts against her skin.

She bathed and changed her clothes, donning a dark outfit and a gray cloak. Then she tended to the wounds on her body. The one on her belly was freshly pink and healed, though her foot still ached. Her hand must be bandaged, which she did before laying down on a plush bed. They would leave before dawn and there was time for a little rest. She threw her arm across her eyes and attempted to sleep. But the nahual was restless, it spun around the room, sniffing at her bloodied hand.

"Give me something to eat. A nibble."

"Don't be a glutton."

"I need it, if I am to help you."

"No," she said, swatting the dog away, half-asleep.

"You had your dinner but I'm not to have mine?"

She felt the dog's narrowed eyes staring at her, felt its spite. "I remember how you left me behind, trapped in a ring, hidden beneath stones. Left me to starve."

"You could have left, leaked into stone and water and out into the world."

"Could I?"

"Are you going to say I'm cruel now?" she asked.

"You've always been cruel. Spiteful and cruel."

And she should have been able to block the memory, but it coursed down her spine like boiling tar. Yalxi wearing the pectoral with the great diamond at its center, sitting atop the pyramid, her hands flat upon her lap and her thoughts simple, forceful: *mine, it is mine. It has been worth it. All of it.* Even Itzyul's death. No remorse, no sorrow, simply triumph as she took her rightful seat.

Mine and mine. From that moment on the world had a different hue.

"You killed your teacher and let your friend die, all for a stone," the nahual whispered. "And now your great love has paid you back with the same coin. I told you so that day, I told you—"

That other memory washed across her body now, that moment when she had taken off the little ring with the pearl. She no longer needed it. Rather than destroy it, though, she hid it away.

"It's what any sorcerer would have done," she said as she stood in the yellow house, in the little room, as she wrapped the ring in a piece of cloth.

Further back, another step into the past, and then Xellah. Young Xellah, at eighteen, the memory so crystalline it made her gasp because she had loved young Xellah with a fierceness that was almost frightening, but also with a tenderness she'd left behind. There, Young Xellah, his lips soft and his breath warm and she wrapping her arms around his neck, trusting her heart to him.

Xellah, who she'd wanted more than any bauble, than any spell. But she'd killed that love in the years henceforth, seeded a field with salt between them.

"I didn't abandon him. He betrayed *me*," she protested.

"Perhaps he did what any sorcerer would have done," the nahual whispered, mocking her and she sat up in bed, whirling out of the fog of memory and staring at the dog which had settled at her side and was glaring at her with bright, yellow eyes.

Time had scrubbed such moments from her mind, time had cleansed the past, but the nahual remembered it for her. That was why it was dangerous. That was why she'd bricked it away.

She shoved the dog off the bed and turned her back to it, but it had once again succeeded in chasing sleep away.

SHE WAS QUIET, her lips pressed tight together, the cloak wrapped snug around her shoulders and a leather satchel with supplies at her feet.

They had boarded one of the skiffs they used around the flower market, quick and nimble and useful when smuggling goods into the city and avoiding import taxes, which meant even if they were caught there was a good chance they could get away, for Yalxi had been provided with a little pouch filled with coins in case a sentry must be bribed. They might think her skiff guilty only of moving contraband. But she was being cautious. The nahual was similarly subdued. There were no quips today, no unpleasant memories. The nahual sat still in its dog shape, while Yalxi laced her hands together and the oarsman maneuvered them through the intricate web of canals.

She held her breath for a moment as they pushed away from the city.

She did not like this, being out there, in the water. The nahual in the diamond had not been partial to water, and neither had been Master Teotah.

The little pearl on her ring had formed in the water and the nahual in it did not mind currents and tides, yet having spent so many years in the presence of the diamond Yalxi now felt displeasure. It was as awkward as being left-handed and being asked to write with her right hand.

Yalxi glanced at the water and thought what might happen if the reach of the Guild of Thieves was narrower than she thought, what if the way was not open to them. There would be nothing left to do but to jump into the water and attempt to swim to shore.

And that terrified her.

Master Teotah had drowned. She could not remember his death, but she knew the facts. Even the nahual could not recall the death: Xellah and Yalxi had scorched the memory clean to protect themselves. But the knowledge lingered and she had feared the water for a long time.

The panicked terror of Teotah's demise had bled into the stone she'd worn against her chest and drilled into her marrow. She did not travel on barges, but on litters. And sometimes, in the middle of the night, she had woken up with a strangled scream in her throat as the pressure of the water threatened to snap her chest in two.

On those nights, in the early years, Xellah had held her close. It was still possible, back then, to find comfort in his embrace, in his body.

The sound of the oar dipping into the water was loud unpleasant, and at last she raised her hands and pressed them against her ears, bowing her head and trying to clear her mind. Before, she'd bitten her hand when faced with the sorcerers and their hounds, the pain bleeding her of logical thought. But this would not do again since it was not spells that she wished to escape, but the chains of the past.

At last the dawn colored the sky and the little skiff reached the edge of the marshes. The oarsman would go no farther.

THE GREEN MARSHLANDS

HER BOOTS SANK into the mud as she slowly made her way across the marsh. In the distance she could see a salt pan, a desolate stretch of land where no plants grew, but she kept away from it, instead plowing in the opposite direction, moving past stubborn roots and little clumps of vegetation. Soft grasses tickled her thighs and the nahual, having turned now into a white butterfly, flew around her head or settled on her hair, which was growing sticky with sweat.

The wind was blowing stronger, tugging at her clothes and threatening a storm. The butterfly became a bird and flew low. They ought to find shelter soon but the world was just mud and water and reeds and grass, with no trees in sight and no sturdy land where to seek refuge.

Yalxi paused and took out the shard of diamond from the pouch, cupping it in her hands until it warmed a little. She felt a gentle tug, nothing but a tiny flicker of power, but it was enough. She changed her course slightly, moving to the right and holding the satchel tight.

"You know, maybe you're fooling yourself and we're going in circles," the nahual said.

"I'd know if that was the case."

"How would you?"

She did not reply. There was no sense in chatting when the nahual was in this mood, bitter because she refused to share her blood. Later, she'd promised, when they made camp, and though it was the sensible thing to do the nahual sulked.

"We should have brought a horse."

"What would you do with a horse here?"

"Eat it," the nahual said simply.

She chuckled and for a while they moved in amicable silence. Then came the patter of light rain, which grew quickly stronger, cold droplets splashing her face as she looked onto the sky. The heavens opened, unleashing a storm.

She kept on walking, the water rising and sometimes reaching below her knees, threatening to pull her down. It was treacherous terrain, and all around there was nothing to see but muddy waters, bits of low scrub and the rain which blinded her way. What had seemed to her a narrow stream that could be waded easily proved to be deeper than she thought. Roots snagged her clothing and she stumbled and fell, panicking for one awful second before she stood up and pressed on.

I refuse to drown, she thought.

The bird dug its claws into her shoulder and screeched at her.

"There, I see something there, to the left."

She turned her head and saw a hill and a dark mass of stones upon it. The nahual yelled something else, but the rain drowned all sounds and the command was clear: head up there. She trudged through green-brown waters, through the treacherous mud and twice slipped, but she pressed up and up until the marshy ground was behind them and she had breathlessly reached the top of the hill.

They stood in front of a little customs house with a thatched roof. It wasn't like the great customs houses that flanked the entrance of the grand causeways of her city, with half a dozen bored sentries dressed in fatigues waiting to examine goods and carts, but one could still make out the symbol above the door, the circle that identified the building as the place where taxes would be collected. The customs house's windows were boarded and it looked abandoned, but there must be a road nearby and in the morning perhaps they would be able to follow it, if they were in luck. For now it was time to rest. She was worn out.

Yalxi opened the door and looked around, finding nothing but old furniture and a fireplace blackened with soot. She inspected a desk that contained old bits of paper, a couple of ledgers. No food nor supplies, and the iron kettle hooks were bare, though logs remained piled by the fireplace and there was a poker on the floor. She picked a few of the logs and lit a fire.

Yalxi took off her cloak and sat in front of the fireplace, warming her hands. When she was sufficiently dry, she took out a strip of salted meat and gnawed at it, then drank from a gourd. The nahual turned into a snake and curled against her side.

She looked at the bandage on her hand, where she'd bitten it, and then pulled her sleeve up and surveyed the tracery of scars upon her skin. Most were old and faint, the product of her own magic-making when she was a girl, since in those days she could not avail herself of the blood of apprentices. But there were still tiny wounds left by Xellah's leeches.

Master Teotah had not bothered with leeches, not towards the end. The obsidian blade sufficed for him. Death was an even more powerful coin than blood.

Amongst the supplies she'd brought on the barge there was a knife, but it was an ordinary one, not for ceremonial use. She'd have to cleanse it with ash and inscribe it if it was to be used in magic making. She knew how to do this, of course. In the beginning, when she'd been nothing but a skinny teenager from nowhere she'd had to make due with as much. Coarse knives and coarse hands and even coarser manners. But she was still worn and tired and didn't want to spend her energy making a weapon, not when she'd ought to be resting and healing. She stuffed the knife back in her satchel.

"Yalxi, will you feed me now?"

"Yes, fine," she muttered and allowed the snake to sink its fangs into her wrist.

The snake nursed itself with her blood and she closed her eyes. She thought of Itzyul and their time apprenticing together, under the watchful eye of Master Teotah. The impressions were not concrete, just fleeting words and moments, bits of the everyday. It was uncomfortable to find herself thinking about her old friend now, like straining to fit into garments she had discarded.

Itzyul had watched over Master Teotah's doves. He kept hundreds of them, for blood magic. Itzyul loved the little birds, she gently stroked their feathers and fed them. Sometimes, when Yalxi had nothing better to do, she helped her friend in the dovecot.

A soft fluttering, the birds cooing, the sun slanting through the windows. This had been their youth.

Wings. Flight. Feathers.

There was a loud bang, like a fist hitting wood, and she opened her eyes and looked at the ceiling. It was still raining, but it had turned into a soft pattering and the fire had morphed into a few crackling embers. The snake had detached itself from Yalxi while she slept and turned into a dog, which lay next to her and sat up, sniffing at the air.

Though her eyes were open now she thought she could still make out the sound of wings. Something was outside, flying, and had perched itself on the roof.

"Yalxi," the nahual whispered.

"Hush," she said and pressed a finger against her lips.

The rain fell steadily, but that was all. For a moment she thought perhaps she'd heard the rumble of thunder and had been confused.

There came three more quick bangs and the flimsy roof of the building was ripped apart and a monstrous bird clawed its way into the room. It resembled a king vulture, as big as a bull, its head streaked bright red and its malicious, hungry eyes fixed on her. And she knew exactly what it hungered for: her blood. Sorcery was like a scent that attracted magical creatures big and small. She had dampened her scent in the city and tricked the hounds, but the bird would not be tricked, this despite the fact that her powers were but a tiny flicker of a flame, nothing but the ghost of a scent.

Yalxi, still weak, the might of her magic drained by pain and constant bleedings, knew for a moment the terrible taste of fright as she grabbed a chair and swung it against the creature's head, trying to frighten it off. The maneuver bought her a minute or two, as the bird bobbed its head up and down, then flapped its wings and charged forward.

She moved aside, quick as she could, pain lancing through her body, and the bird crashed into an armoire, then turned quickly around and stared at her again. Its ugly, black tongue slipped out of its beak as if it were already savoring the taste of her flesh.

She had heard of beasts like this, monstrosities that had roamed the world before it had become this world, when the land had been primordial, a sketch of itself, and they had feasted on the bones and skin of men. Whether this thing had found her out of its own volition or whether perhaps this was Xellah's doing, she did not know, but either way it was a night of black luck for her since she was ill-prepared for a fight of this sort.

But she had not endured days and nights in a windowless cell, nor the agony of the leeches, for this creature to have her as its meal. So she ducked and hid under a table and yelled to the nahual.

"The poker!"

The dog ran to the fire place and the bird dashed towards her again, its claws ready. It began pecking at the table with its enormous beak, sending splinters flying into the air, but the table was finely made, unlike the roof, and resisted the attack for a couple of minutes.

The dog came running to her, the poker in its mouth, and she grabbed the piece of metal just as the bird bit a great chunk of table away and spit it out, destroying the flimsy barrier that had lay between them.

The bird stared at her again, almost slobbering in its delight, when the dog bit at its tail. Outraged, the bird turned its head and hissed at the nahual. At that angle, with its head turned, Yalxi was able to perfectly see the great black eye of the bird, like an obsidian mirror, and her own face reflected in it. She swung the poker hard, driving the metal point into the eye.

The bird let out a thunderous screech and Yalxi grasped a broken table leg, ready to smash that against the bird's head should it come near her, but in its pain it began to flap its wings and flew up into the air, disappearing into the night.

Yalxi, crouching on the floor, held onto the table leg and stared at the tattered roof, but the bird did not return. Nevertheless, she did not sleep again. The dog, too, remained alert.

In the morning she pocketed a fistful of ashes from the fireplace and some writing instruments: a bottle of ink, a quill. She even took a rusted nail. Then she found the path that ran by the customs house. It was old and overgrown, but better than nothing, and since it aligned with the direction the diamond shard was pointing to, they followed it.

When the sun was high above their heads they stopped by the side of the road and Yalxi opened her satchel and ate more salted meat. Then she took out the knife and rubbed it with ash. She used the nail to carefully carve a glyph on the wooden pommel, then the ink and the quill to write symbols on the blade, symbols that she then wiped away. It was crude work but it was never the beauty of a ceremonial knife that made it effective. It was about willpower and need and desire. She still had those.

Yet, would that be enough? She hoped to challenge Xellah to a duel, but this would not be like the mock duels of their youth when they sparred and laughed. Besides, she wasn't even sure where she was sitting at this exact point and time. The diamond guided her and she followed blindly.

I refuse to fail, she thought even if she wondered how far they'd have to go. She had no memory of this road, there were no markers which might help her gauge the journey. All she knew, as they walked, was an intense and terrible desolation. She might not be able to remember the manner and location of Teotah's death, but she could feel the memory of the death in her bones. It was like an old, festering wound.

When they rested on the side of the road, though, she didn't think about her old Master. She thought instead about Itzyul and lay there, with the dog curled against her belly, her eyes open while the animal slept. As soon as the sun began rising in the horizon, she got up and nudged the nahual.

They diamond shard was warm against her hand and the stone road beneath their feet was really a carpet of weeds rather than a road. But she didn't doubt they were on the right track and late in the day they reached a copse of tall trees. The trees were arranged around a lake rimmed with reeds and blanketed with water lilies, their twisted roots dipping into the waters. And those waters had a curious color: they were black, like tar.

Yalxi crouched on the root of a tree. It was quiet there. She could hear no birds, only the humming of insects. The white dog sniffed the air and growled.

"There's foul magic here."

Indeed. The remains of Teotah's power lingered, caking the water. It was an almost imperceptible infection.

"Then we're at the right place," Yalxi said. "Awake and hear me, Teotah. Awake and grant me an audience."

But the waters of the lake remained still and her legs began to cramp as she sat there, crouched by the shore, waiting. Finally, recognizing nothing else would do, she slammed her hand against a jagged rock, reinjuring herself and drawing fresh blood. Then she held the tiny shard of diamond tight in her fist before tossing it into the water.

It flew through the air, covered in blood, like a red spark, and sank into the pond.

It was as if the lake drew in a deep breath, the water suddenly rippling and the water lilies shivering. The dog barked.

From the water there rose a voice that was not a real voice, for the speaker had no lungs, no mouth, it was thought made audible through the limbs of the trees and the petals of the lilies.

"Yalxi, you dare to return," the voice said. It rumbled through the copse, like thunder.

And for a second she recalled fear. The terror of uncertainty, of never knowing whether Master Teotah might demand she be bled dry that evening, or instead he might shower her with praise. He could be a tyrant and also a kind father. One could not tell. But as ambition clouded his eyes, more and more he turned to violence until the three of them could stand it no longer.

She became that scared young woman, scarcely twenty-one, who had quivered when she heard the sorcerer's voice.

She immediately hated herself for this, for the chill running down her spine and the sudden weakness in her limbs.

This was the spirit's fault! It had brought back the memories and feelings of the old Yalxi with it. She was helpless, small and young and that was *not* her. It had not been her for a very long time because she had buried that Yalxi together with the ring of pearl.

She stood up and stared at the water.

"I've come, yes."

"My diamond…what have you done with my diamond?" Teotah asked and she felt the root of the tree beneath her feet softly vibrating, as though it were alive. She jumped onto a rock as the root whipped up and down, like a frenzied snake before laying still again.

"Don't attempt that again," she said. "I'm beyond your reach."

Teotah let out an angry rumble and the lake shivered, water lilies wilting, but it was coarse magic. Just the dregs of power and though Teotah's might was so considerable that he lingered like a jagged scar on the land, it was not the sort of magic that could harm a sorcerer with half a brain. The bits of power that remained, the bits of Teotah, were too sluggish and brutish to think much of anything through, but they hungered and she needed that hunger.

"Now, be civil and I'll be civil in return. Will you be civil?" she asked and tiptoed onto another rock. "I'll tell you what happened to the diamond if you are."

"Tell."

"Xellah has it. He's betrayed me. I won't detail my fall, amusing as you might find it; there is no point. It should suffice to say I wish to have my revenge on him. I want to get the diamond back and for that I need your help."

"I want to taste your flesh," Teotah whispered.

"No. You want the diamond back and Xellah has it and he is invincible. Or he thinks he is. But if you assist me, I'll bring him here and you can have the diamond back. You can have Xellah, too. You may feast upon *his* flesh."

"You are a traitor," Teotah said and again the roots from the trees twitched.

"We are all traitors. You taught me that. Take everything you want, you said. Well, I want Xellah dead and I care only for that. The diamond is yours."

Teotah laughed and what a terrible laughter it was; putrid, ancient and laced with an unquenchable hunger. Teotah must have the jewel. And Teotah in turn must have recognized her own need, her blind commitment to revenge.

"Yes, I taught you and so did my diamond heart. You'll have your revenge. You will bring me Xellah. Now, dip your hand in the water."

She looked down, at the dark pond that did not return her reflection, the lilies like a shroud upon the surface. You could not tell what lay beneath no matter how hard you peered at the water.

"Don't be foolish, he can't be trusted," the nahual quickly whispered.

Again she felt like a lost child, but she shook her head—stubbornness and anger cutting deeper than fear—and thrust her hand into the water. She glimpsed, for the first time, something beneath the surface. It was pale, undefined, and she felt something slippery and cold slide against her fingers.

Whatever brushed her hand, it was dead, and it clasped her tight, threatening to tip her into the lake. Yet she did not pull back, still holding out her hand. What else could she do? She'd come this far.

The dog whined.

Whatever held her tight pressed something against her palm and let her go. Yalxi pulled her hand out of the water and held a clump of mud and plants from the bottom of the pond. Trapped between the roots of the plants, caked with dirt, were thirteen teeth. Despite their time submerged under water they looked white and perfect.

The teeth almost seemed to smile at her as she cupped them between her hands.

"Yalxi, throw them back," the nahual said. "This is necromancy and worse than that."

She placed the teeth in the pouch hanging from her neck and broke a reed that grew by the pond. "It is done," she muttered, to steady herself and wash any lingering misgivings away.

WHITE TEETH

THE CITY SEEMED farther away upon their return and perhaps it was, some sorcery having allowed her to reach the lake faster than might have been possible by an ordinary mortal. Or perhaps she was simply tired and now dragged her feet slowly.

The nahual was morose. She had expected it to again acquire the shape of a dog and gambol through the grass, but instead it remained curled up inside her ring. It stretched out one night, becoming an iguana, pale as ivory.

"We'll be in the city tomorrow."

"I suppose we will," she said.

"I thought you might have desisted by now."

"When I have Teotah's teeth around my neck?"

"Precisely because you have his teeth around your neck. It's carrion and it's festered magic, Yalxi. You know as well as me it is a folly to play with dead things."

"I have no other choice. Are you scared now?"

They were resting under the shade of a poplar tree, Yalxi's back was against the trunk. The iguana crawled upon her lap and stared at her face.

"I always feared your power."

"And delighted in it."

"You've shone as bright as a star. But your rage clouds your thoughts, just like ambition blinded Teotah. Should you succeed and annihilate Xellah, then you will have to contend with Teotah."

"Teotah is but bones and a few teeth."

"And with only those scraps he has lingered upon the land. I have not felt such enduring power ever before. You are toying with tremendous forces, and I cannot protect you."

"As if you ever could! If you have ever wondered why I put you aside it is because you are the ring of a carnival magician, of a child."

The iguana slid onto the ground and turned into vapor, and then the vapor drew into the ring. She felt it against her skin, not hot with anger, but cold with sorrow. She bit her lip with a pang of regret and let out a sigh.

"I am sorry," she said. "That was unkind."

But the nahual did not reply. She missed the warmth of the dog next to her and the thin blanket wrapped around her body provided scant comfort. She found herself thinking of her youth again. This time, it was out of her own volition, not a memory thrust before her by the nahual who sought to taunt her, but her own inquiry into the past.

She thought back to those first days when she had joined Teotah's entourage. Those had been times of sweetness and optimism. Then their master had changed, grown darker. Or perhaps in the beginning Yalxi had simply been content to ignore his darkness, his thirst.

After all, sorcery requires blood. Who was she to judge him?

But then, in whispered conversations, the three of them had voiced that inevitable truth: their Master was mad. They had discussed a course of action and though all were in agreement that something must be done, they differed on the appropriate course. Itzyul had proposed a rather blunt solution, but one which would have meant the destruction of the diamond. Yalxi would not hear of it. After all, she'd reasoned, the power of the diamond might be used for other means.

Xellah had backed her, as he naturally did, and Itzyul, outnumbered, had agreed to that more dangerous course. And now, under the shadow of the poplar tree, with the ring on her finger and the teeth pressed against her chest, Yalxi remembered the whole thing, the murder, from beginning to end.

Drowning. Water. Because the spirit in the diamond feared water. So they had cunningly lured their Master to that pond—they had secured a ruse, an appropriate enticement—and set themselves on him.

There had been that moment when Itzyul had a chance to crush the diamond, the burn it into ashes, but Yalxi had stopped her. Yalxi had said no, you must not!

The girl obeyed.

She paid with her life for that.

Afterwards, when they'd succeeded in murdering Master Teotah, his body sinking into the pond, Xellah had pulled Itzyul's battered body from the shore, where it lay amongst the reeds. As he bent over the young woman, in grief, Yalxi had pulled something else from amongst the twisted branches of the trees and the reeds. Something infinitely more valuable: the diamond pectoral that had belonged to their master. And even as Itzyul lay dying there and Xellah sank to his knees and clutched her hand, Yalxi's one thought was for the diamond.

Yalxi put on the pectoral as her best friend died on the shore of that pond. Xellah turned his face towards her and he said "Yalxi?"

Her name, intimate and warm. A name spoken countless nights when they lay in the dark, in the quiet of the yellow house and later in the pyramid. Whispered, her name, the softest of promises.

"Mistress Yalxi," she said, feeling neither sorrow nor doubt. "The Sorcerers' Guild is mine."

Now, under the poplar, a tear ran down her cheek and she wiped it with the palm of her hand. The nahual had been right. Yalxi lied prettily. She didn't need the fullness of the memory to know that, but it hurt to taste her deceit so fully.

While escaping the city had taken much effort, her return was simple. She joined a group of peasants who were walking down a causeway, intent on selling their wares. Her clothes, dirtied during the journey, and her dark hair lank and falling across her face, rendered her common, unworthy of any notice.

Once inside the city she walked to the neighborhood of the paper sellers, where both the makers of bark paper, which was used in magic-making, and the sellers of ordinary paper goods made their living. She bought sheets of bark paper, wax, and other materials. She secured a room nearby. The paper quarter was not so fine that a scrawny, poorly dressed woman would stand out and no one looked at her askance. On the top floor of an inn that tended to house paper merchants from small villages she spread her belongings.

Sorcery did not require the cover of the night, but it did help, so she waited until the moon was out and then she lit a couple of candles. Then she grabbed the reed she had taken from the pond and the knife, and began shaping it into a blowgun. When she was done she pricked a finger and gathered her blood in a small dish.

She began drawing the symbols of power that would be required. It was slow, painstaking work. If she'd had the diamond, she could have simply traced crude glyphs and be done with it, the might of the diamond amplifying her own magic. But with only the nahual from the pearl ring to assist her, she must pay more attention, and permeate each stroke with her willpower.

Sticks of incense burned as she worked, whispering words with as much vehemence as an apprentice who has only begun weaving spells. And in truth, she did feel rather new, scrubbed clean. She didn't like it. It was too much like being naked, but there was no way around it.

At first the nahual did not care much for her work. It stubbornly hid inside the ring, but eventually it stretched out in the shape of a cat and circled her with interest as she wrapped the bark paper around the blowgun and began applying the lacquer. When she was done the cat bumped its head against her hands and she scratched the animal's head.

SHE SLEPT FOR a whole day afterwards, her body recovering from the spell-making. Her bones ached when she rose from bed and as she stared at her face in a mirror hanging above the washbasin, it was ever so obvious why sorcerers used jewels and nahuales to assist them.

Under her eyes there were dark circles and numerous strands of gray adorned her hairline, stark against her ebony tresses. Her face was not thin, it was outright bony. If she'd had the diamond, she might have hidden these flaws with ease. Now she must contend with the reality of a body that had deteriorated with the onslaught of spellcasting and had been further mangled by her treatment in Xellah's dungeons.

"Don't feel bad about it. Neither one of us is looking our best," the cat said. "Though you should eat more. Your blood is thin."

"Aren't you picky?" she said, but smiled. "Come, let's fetch me supper and listen to gossip."

"My two favorite things."

A few blocks from her lodgings Yalxi found a tavern with a diverse and numerous clientele. Paper merchants and workers, but also tradespeople of other sort and even a couple of barge owners who ferried goods down the canals. She ordered food and drink, and sat herself in a corner. Once again her ordinariness was the best disguise. Reduced as she was, she posed no threat, provided no temptation. She even felt that Xellah had given up his search of her, that the hounds had been called in. For good measure, she would move to a new place in the morning, but she suspected her hunch was true.

After an hour and a couple of bowls of broth accom-panied with chunks of bread, she heard the gossip she'd come for. Two rat catchers were lamenting their current situation, complaining to a woman who ran an orphanage and arranged to hire out some of the children there for various and sundry tasks. The Sorcerers' Guild had of late increased the quota of rats it needed. At first this was a boon to the rat catchers but now the number of rats they wanted was rather high and the rat catchers could scarcely keep up with the demands.

This was what Yalxi suspected would come to pass. Master Teotah had followed a similar pattern, first requiring more rats, then dogs, then common lowlifes, and finally his apprentices. Blood was a common coin for sorcerers—and jokes about leeches kept many an apprentice in good humor—but Teotah employed it as though there was an unending source of it rather than being a precious resource. Xellah would do the same. He was probably growing frustrated by now, especially since he'd lost Yalxi and her blood, which, despite whatever the nahual might say about it being thin, was much more enticing than that of young students with little experience in the magic arts.

"I have already hired another two boys to help with the rats, this on top of my two nephews and my son," said one of the rat catchers. "I'm running out of hands and one can't just find a decent rat catcher around every corner, not when the guild won't take rats that are dead."

"If they were buying the tails it'd be no problem," said a second rat catcher. "But live ones? That's the problem, you see."

"It's not the kind of work the children normally do, though," the woman said. "What if the rats were to bite them? Who would pay for their treatment?"

"Not much chance of that if they wear thick gloves. Come, now, the Master Sorcerer is going on a procession in just a few days and he needs the rats."

A procession. How wonderful. Yalxi paid for her meal and departed. Here and there she asked a question, to the beggars and the drunkards and the other riffraff she encountered as she slowly wove her way back to her lodging, and pieced together the details she required. The day, the time, the route, the procession would take.

In the morning she left the old room she'd been renting and found a new one on a street parallel to the path of the procession and another further away, on an alleyway lined with butcher shops.

She bought a change of clothes, purchased two pig carcasses that were promptly delivered at an appointed hour, and spent the next couple of days exploring the area between both of the places she was renting. The buildings were close together in this quarter and in some alleyways the poorest denizens of the city had built themselves illegal wooden shacks, making the streets almost impassable.

She circled the neighborhood, sucking on an orange she'd bought from a street seller while taking careful note of the buildings, the streets, the businesses.

Then she timed herself walking briskly through the streets, seeing how fast one might move between both lodgings.

"You do know your right foot still aches, don't you?" the nahual, in its cat shape, asked. "You're not exactly going to be fast right now."

"My right foot always aches," she said, dismissive. "It's an old wound."

"Perhaps, but let's discuss the rest of your plan. Challenging Xellah is a folly, especially when he'll be surrounded by so many attendants. You have, what? The blood of two pigs?"

The nahual hadn't complained about the pig's blood the previous evening, when she sliced them and collected it, dipping her newly acquired knife in it and then drinking from it. She'd let the nahual drink too. It could not provide the same nourishment as human blood, but it was a treat.

"You have little faith in me."

"My faith is sufficient, but my common sense is greater."

"I can't sneak into his rooms in the middle of the night. I must challenge him and he must come to me."

"You don't have a blade for a duel."

Yalxi patted the knife dangling from a coarse leather belt.

"That is no proper blade. You could gut fish with that."

"Or a man," she said with a shrug.

"And you think he will duel with you?" the nahual asked, amused.

"He must, after I have humiliated him. Now, let me think. I must plan every detail of this and block their path."

"Plans don't always go the way we want them too."

"Were you always this annoying?" she asked, picking up the cat and cradling it in her arms.

"Your ambition and my common sense were always a good combination."

She chuckled and scratched the cat's chin, then kept walking until they reached a rickety wooden bridge and a canal. "I'm sorry I left you behind," she said, looking at the bridge.

"What? An honest apology?"

"You'll make me regret it?"

"Never."

They were both quiet, listening to the sounds of the canal, the water licking a boat that was tied up ahead. The nahual spoke again. "You were correct that I could have simply left The Yellow House, found myself a new abode. But I was waiting for you to come back."

"Don't say that."

"But it's true. I'm very fond of you, for all your monstrous flaws, and wouldn't want to see you dead by the hand of a vulgar mage like Xellah. Which is why I caution you."

"Vulgar!"

"You have remarkably poor taste when it comes to some things."

"You're remarkably rude for a cat."

"My dear, all cats are rude. And that pimply youth can't have grown to become anything more than a boorish man."

She chuckled again and set the nahual down. They crossed the bridge together, walking side by side.

As she stood on a balcony, dressed in white linen, leaning forward and surveying the street below, she had to admit the nahual was correct. Xellah *was* vulgar. Yalxi had also marched in processions. Sometimes, it became necessary to demonstrate your might, especially when meeting with certain recalcitrant lords. She did not dispute the role of pageantry. But Xellah's retinue seemed to her wildly overblown. Oh, there were the usual guards and attendants and the ceremonial litter. But Xellah had decided to have musicians during his procession. They shook rattles and blew a horn, and behind them there came a coterie of halberdiers that went beyond the usual number. Half a dozen ought to have been enough. Xellah had instead engaged around fifteen guards. Did he fear for his life? Yalxi doubted it. It was a show of power.

As the litter drifted closer to her balcony she was able to have a clear look at the sorcerer. He was dressed in gaudy crimson robes, stitched with jewels, and across his chest there lay the breastplate with the diamond. He had a headdress with enormous feathers and rings on his fingers and a golden staff, all of which were completely unnecessary, in her opinion, for a procession of this sort. What was he celebrating, after all? That he was meeting with one of the dukes who lived in one of their white palaces?

She watched Xellah, sitting in his litter, his hands resting on his chair and his head held up high. A beam of light caught on the diamond resting on his chest. She raised the blowgun, inserted a tooth in the opening, and sent the projectile flying in the direction of Xellah's face.

It caught him in the cheek and Xellah yelped. She had a few seconds to savor her triumph and delight in his startled face. His lips moved and she couldn't hear what he was telling his attendants but she could imagine it well enough.

The diamond was supposed to make the wearer invincible to ordinary weapons.

Of course, the tooth was not ordinary. It had cut Xellah's cheek, leaving a thin line of crimson.

Someone raised an arm, pointing her out, tracing the trajectory of the projectile. She stood there, her hands closed around the iron railing of the balcony and stared at Xellah and he stared back at her, his dark eyes growing incensed. He yelled and she picked up her leather satchel and hurried to the roof of the building.

She moved quick, then jumped onto the roof of the neighboring house. It was simple. Everything was so crowded together that it was but a small leap. Her feet pounded over rickety wooden huts and took her above tenements, following the path she had carefully traced in the days before the procession. The cat ran behind her, quick as her own shadow.

She kept moving, from wooden huts to houses with adobe roofs. There was a wider gap between buildings here and her lungs were burning. Below, on the streets, she heard men bellowing, shoving people away, attempting to catch up with her. But it was faster to move on the rooftops than try to elbow her way through the crowds, and so she had a sliver of an advantage.

She pressed on, because there was no stopping now and the bridge was almost there. After the bridge she would be able to slow down. She closed a hand into a fist, feeling the band of silver around her finger, drawing on the power of the nahual to propel herself forward.

She jumped down to a balcony and then another, until she reached street level.

There ahead was the rickety wooden bridge over the canal. And she ran across, her feet thundering and making the bridge quake. When she reached the other side she traced a glyph in the air, then knelt down and pressed her hands against the wooden planks, which began to smolder. It burnt lightning quick, glowing red like a hot coal and turning into ash. It only took a few beats of her anxious heart and it was done.

She dashed down an alley and stood there, her back against the wall. Gods! She hadn't worked this hard since she was a girl and every muscle in her body protested. She brushed a hand across her face, pulling stray hairs back into place, and began walking again. But no sooner had she exited the alley onto a little plaza with a fountain that she found herself standing before three men with yellow cloaks.

So much for blocking their path, she thought.

Three. She had a satchel on her shoulder and a little knife at her hip. Nevertheless, she held her head up high and spoke with a strong voice, like she would have done in the pyramid's throne room.

"I'll let you turn back unharmed now and you may give a message to Xellah," she said. "I caution you: It'll be best if you obey me."

"You're not our Master anymore for us to obey you," said one of the sorcerers.

"And you're not my pupils. I'll strike you down if you attempt to touch me."

But they didn't heed her. Why would they? They saw a tired woman with no real weapons and one of them walked forward, twin daggers inscribed with glyphs in his hands and a cocky smile plastered on his face. Youth who knew no fear. Yalxi had no time for them.

She sighed. "Bite," she ordered.

The young man frowned, confused. The confusion turned to horror as the little alley cat that had been trailing her leapt into the air, turned into a dog, savaging the man's leg. It wasn't a very big dog since neither the nahual in the pearl nor Yalxi had quite recovered their full strength, but it had teeth and it used them well.

The other two sorcerers were shocked by attack. One of them tried to pull the dog off, the other turned to her. Yalxi punched him with no finesse, simple desperation taking over. When she'd fought with Xellah it had been with panache, it had been a display of pageantry. But she had no inclination for that now and a rough blow served her fine.

The young man perhaps expected a more sophisticated attack and seemed truly surprised to get punched in the face and even more shocked when she kicked him, making him lose his balance. The man fell with a thunderous groan and she jumped atop him, pressing her knife against his chest and drawing blood. Then she spit at him, traced a glyph in the air.

Yalxi turned her head to find the two sorcerers had managed to wrestle the dog away and were moving in her direction. But her hand was pressed against the man's chest and her knife was slick with blood, slick with stolen sorcerous power, the blade growing incandescent.

She threw the knife in their direction and missed. It fell with a clang behind the men, bouncing off the edge of the fountain. The men guffawed, amused.

"Give me fire," she said.

And then she smiled. A long rope of fire, from the point where the knife had fallen to where Yalxi was standing rose in the air. Both men were standing in its path and both men were singed, their hair and clothes bursting into flames. They ran, screaming, one of them dashing blindly in the direction of the nearby canal, the other tossing himself into the fountain.

The air smelled of sulphur and magic.

She opened the satchel, took out a piece of bark paper and placed it in the palm of the sorcerer on the ground. "Give this to Xellah," she said.

Then she picked up her knife and motioned to the dog, who was busy licking the blood that had spilled on the ground. They followed winding streets, and as they walked she took out the black cape she had stuffed inside the satchel and put it on. Thus attired she'd be harder to spot. But she didn't think there would be anyone to spot her.

Their pace was quick, her body thrummed with energy. The blood was invigorating and the fight, though unwanted, revived her somewhat. The dog next to her trotted merrily at her side.

They reached their abode above the butcher's shop without further delays. Inside, she had another pig carcass ready. She doubted it would be necessary, but she still sliced its neck and dipped her knife in the blood while the dog feasted.

She lay on a chair, watching the nahual eat, while she touched the leather bag hanging from her neck, rolling back and forth the teeth inside.

"You think he will really face you alone?" the nahual asked after it had its fill.

"Master Teotah would."

"He is not Teotah."

"But he wishes he was. And the diamond…it may compel him. The diamond may want to reunite with Teotah."

"I still think we should let this be and simply run off into the world. I'm feeling a lot stronger and you're healing nicely. But ultimately do we want to get into a fight with an all-powerful sorcerer and risk our necks when we could be headed in the opposite direction? Facing against apprentices is one thing, but a true sorcerer—"

"Rest. We'll leave in the morning," she said.

The nahual groaned in protest but there was nothing to discuss. She hadn't come this far to slink away in shame. And there was the diamond to consider. Always that diamond, invading her thoughts.

Yalxi was cautious as they left the city. There was no need to hide in a barge, but she walked down the causeway, the knife within easy reach.

The nahual was correct, it was not the fine blade of a sorcerer, but it was indeed appropriate for gutting fish and men, should one of them attempt to block her way. Although she felt a twinge of apprehension—she was not really back to her old self—she shrugged it off and counted on Xellah's ego to open the way to her.

He'd want to measure up to her, now that she'd proven wilier than he'd anticipated.

He'd always liked a challenge. It's the reason why he'd loved her in the first place.

"Don't sell yourself short. It wasn't the only reason," the nahual said. It was a pale beetle, resting on the pommel of the knife.

"What do you know?" she replied. She didn't feel like putting up with his jokes.

But the nahual kept talking. "You were talented and girlishly pretty and—"

She smirked. "Girlish! That is what you recall."

"And *decent*, Yalxi. You had a sense of fairness. Xellah admired you for that and Teotah feared you for the same reason."

She didn't know what to say to that and pulled the cloak tighter around her body as they exited the city.

BLACK HEART

THE JOURNEY BACK to the pond was uneventful. No thundering rains or strange beasts barred her path. The nahual grew tired of its beetle shape and became a white dog. It chased a flock of birds and they flew into the sky. She watched them and thought of Itzyul and her doves.

How soft she had been, Itzyul. Soft and gentle. Perhaps Yalxi had once been decent, but she had never been gentle. Her way was the hard way; she'd been whetted by hardships. And now she thought of the coldness of the diamond against her fingers, the spirit inside filling her veins with power.

It was what she'd always wanted. In its faceted depths she knew hunger and completion.

When they arrived by the lake it was late in the evening. The aquatic lilies had all died and the waters were murky, a thin film of green covering the surface, like a membrane. Everything felt dead and blasted in this spot, but she could sense no immediate trace of power, as she'd done last time. It was the natural death of all things; it was an ugly pond with ugly twisted trees.

If you prodded and poked beneath this veneer of normality you could sense something rotten, but it took a little while to taste the foulness. Teotah was sleeping, he was concealing himself.

She marked a spot by a gnarled tree and hid her bag with provisions underneath. Then she leaned against the trunk and took out the blowgun, twirling it between her fingers. Around her neck hung the remaining twelve teeth. They clacked softly when she moved and made an awful kind of music.

When the sky had turned purple and the moon rose in the sky, a figure came walking amongst the trees. He was dressed in yellow and carried daggers with jewels on their hilt. On his chest rested a pectoral and in the center an incomparable diamond, shining so bright you'd think it a star from the heavens. The man moved slowly, he walked like a king. But she grinned because she remembered him as a callow youth who stole coins from the patrons at the drinking dens when he needed the money.

Xellah, decked in finery, brimming with stolen power, but she knew him and was not dazzled.

He stopped a few paces from Yalxi and regarded her in silence. He'd come without attendants, just as she'd expected. He was angry and wished to finish her in silence, to toss her bones into an unmarked spot and be done with her.

"Well, won't you greet me?" she asked. "Have you lost your manners?"

"Not at all. When I saw you in the city I thought you a vengeful ghost and I am still surprised, that is all."

"You couldn't have expected me to simply slither away, could you?"

"Why not? It would have been the most logical choice."

"Perhaps for you."

"Duels are such needless formalities. Once upon a time you might have agreed with me. Why bother with senseless spectacle when a clever knife will do?"

"I never thought duels were needless formalities."

"If we duel I shall kill you," he said. It did not sound like a warning. It sounded like fact and her heart, blackened and shrunk and smoldering, beat hard with rage, but she pressed her lips together and smiled at him.

"Maybe not. Perhaps I'm prepared. After all, I always knew you'd betray me."

"Yes, that was exactly the problem," he muttered and he looked a little hurt, but then he scoffed and looked at the lake. "What a sight. Our Master's final resting place. Did you have to swim for a long time in that disgusting water before finding the teeth?"

The diamond caught a stray beam of light, shining, almost winking at her. "Not too long."

He kicked a pebble into the lake. It fell with a loud splash, made ripples. Then it was all terribly quiet, just the wind brushing against the branches of the trees. He couldn't discern the rancidness of the land. He was not subtle, he had always been a little blunt. It served her purposes, now.

He looked at her. "It won't make a difference, you know? Not as long as I wear the diamond."

"Then you better hold on to it tight."

"I'll give you a decent burial, Yalxi. You deserve as much," he said.

"I accept your challenge."

"As I do yours."

He was upon her quickly, pulling out his daggers and throwing himself at the sorceress. Hot-headed. He was always hot-headed, he did not think things through while she plotted and planned. Even when he'd betrayed Yalxi it had been a blunt attack. And he was blunt once again as they fought, assuming he'd win by sheer use of force. He was stronger than her, thanks to the diamond, and she was still paper-thin, the shadow of her own self.

But she'd dueled with him many times before, when they were young. They had fought and practiced and laughed. She knew his favorite method of attack, this was a dance with predictable steps. So she blocked him instantly and he came at her again but again she evaded him.

They went like this for a while. At first he was amused, probably expecting a quick end to the fight. But when she jumped back, when she dashed across rocks and feinted and whirled away, when it was obvious he was only tiring himself and despite the pitiful knife in her hands Yalxi could move, could think fast, his face went from amused to angry.

He stopped with the simple attacks and spoke a furious word, traced a symbol in the air.

A shadow emerged from the diamond on his chest. It was violet-black, and seemed to glow a little, as if it were made of burnt embers, and it had two eyes that were bright as jewels. The shadow became a monstrous beast. It had scales like a crocodile, but its limbs were the long, agile limbs of a frog and its maw was filled with razor-sharp teeth. It roared, a primal and cruel sound, rushing towards her.

It was the nahual from the diamond, which had once done her bidding.

She rolled desperately away and the monster crashed against a tree. But there, to the left, was Xellah all of a sudden, slashing at her arm. She managed to evade him, but the sting of his blade made her wince and the crocodile was coming for her again.

Yalxi scrambled behind a tree, took out her blowgun and released two projectiles. The teeth hit the monster in the head and it roared in anger, its tail violently thumping against the ground. Xellah, however, was uninjured and he clashed against her once more, his daggers flashing through the air, and Yalxi was able to repel him, but there—again. Another cut, this to her side, and she was hardly able to evade a slice to her throat before she threw herself flat on the ground.

That maneuver surprised Xellah and she pressed the blowgun against her lips, once again sending two projectiles into the air. They hit Xellah square in the chest and he groaned as loudly as the beast had just a few seconds before, tottering and stepping back.

It was no longer a well-practiced dance, but frenetic fight for survival as she alternated between tossing projectiles in one direction and another. She could hardly breathe, her lungs were aflame and if the crocodile monster should get a hold of her, he'd tear her to shreds.

So she ran, kept going in circles. Xellah was growing more confident, cocky even, her futile attempts to evade him amused him. He caught her again, managed to slice at her ribs, at her mid-section. The wounds were shallow but she was growing dizzy and he was chuckling. The nahual from the diamond seemed amused too. Rather than chase her, it had ceased its pursuit and sat grinning and watching her.

She'd tire soon.

She'd be done soon.

She was slowing down, she was staggering. Her legs were getting heavier.

Round and round they went, she tossed a projectile, then another. When she had only one tooth left he gave her the brightest smile, like a blade.

They stood at the edge of the lake. She panted and tried to keep steady on her legs. From the corner of her eye she could see the crocodile-beast crawling forward, ready to snap her bones in two.

"I'm so sorry," Xellah said.

"I am too," she whispered and she said a word and traced a symbol.

Her nahual leapt from the ring and became a white bird that flew at Xellah's face. The sorcerer raised his hands, furious, shoving it away. It was then, as he was momentarily distracted by the clumsy attack, that she tossed the final tooth in his direction and hit him square in the chest. Hit the diamond and let the blowgun fall to the ground.

The crocodile shivered and Xellah got the bird off him with a quick slash of the knife before staring at her with fury, a scratch from the bird's claws painting his cheek crimson.

"Is that it?" he yelled. "Have you had enough?"

The tooth was now embedded in the diamond but Xellah was otherwise unharmed and she was out of projectiles. With the blade alone, with her small nahual, she could cause but the slightest damage. They both knew it and Xellah shook his head.

"You're foolish," he said.

Behind him the dark, still lake did not seem so still anymore. She spied ripples extending across the surface.

"Not as much as you."

She took a deep breath, dropped her knife and then hurtled forward, no finesse to the attack, simply tossing herself at him with such force that she managed to surprise him and they both fell into the water with a mighty splash.

This was her most terrifying fear, the most dreadful death she could envision. Dungeons did not scare her and torture could be endured, yet the mere idea of being entombed in a watery grave made her want to gag.

But in they went, sinking into the waters.

Xellah shoved her away quickly and she did not resist, she could not hold him even if she tried. He began swimming up, towards the surface.

Something flashed beneath them. It was white and it spread up, like a tendril or the arm of an octopus. The scent of death and menace was suddenly thick around them. Xellah looked down, confused. Neither of them could see what was beneath the water but they could both feel something stretching and waking up.

It was old and hungry and the tooth had clanged against the diamond, summoning it like a guest might be called for dinner.

They swam back up to the surface. Xellah moved quick but before his head could bob out of the water something pale had wrapped itself around one of his legs. Up close she was able to see what it was made of. It wasn't the arm of an octopus, nor a tendril. It looked like a rope. Instead of fibers, it had been woven with bones and pale, deceased tissue.

And there was a stench to it, even though she couldn't possibly smell anything at that moment. The flower of decay in bloom, the touch of old, calcified power.

It was what remained of Master Teotah, existing, waiting, in the bottom of this pond with simmering rage and bitterness. Waiting for the moment when he would rise again.

Another tendril wrapped itself around Xellah, then another.

The sorcerer was now screaming, trying desperately to summon assistance but his words were muffled by the waters, then came the whip of yet another tendril tight against his mouth quieting him utterly—and even if his nahual had been able to hear him, maybe he would not have obeyed.

Because here now was the true master of the diamond, hoping to reunite with his lost treasure.

She kicked her legs as quick as she could and fought upward, until her head jutted out of the water and gasped a mouthful of air. The crocodile beast was nowhere to be seen and she could, if she hurried, be away from this place before Master Teotah was done with Xellah.

It was the most logical choice and for one interminable moment she thought to follow this instinct. Then she took a second, furious gulp of air, and sank back under the water. She forced her limbs to obey her, forced herself to think of nothing and swim down, down, until she caught a flash of whiteness again.

The ropes of dead tissue and bone almost seemed to glow, pearlescent, as she approached them. Xellah's eyes were closed and the two thick tendrils had wrapped around his legs and reached his waist and the third was at his throat, squeezing him tight. There was no hope that she might cut him loose, even if she'd still had her knife.

Twined as Xellah was, the pectoral and the diamond were still clearly visible, nothing had wrapped around his chest. She swam closer to him, her hands brushing the piece of metal.

Another tendril was rising, threatening to catch Yalxi. She felt it tugging at her ankle and she shut her eyes, pleading silently for just a single chance. And she bit into the index finger on her right hand. She bit clean through it—through skin and bone, fuelled by what could only be called madness—and let the blood coat her tongue before kissing the ring of pearl and pressing her left palm against the diamond.

Give me fire, she demanded.

It was not a command spoken. It was *felt*. The highest sort of magic one could command, no longer bound to words, knives or glyphs, but the simple most arcane form of sorcery: blood and willpower.

The nahual joined her, warm inside the pearl ring, then searing hot, her hand crackling. The tendrils that had wrapped around her legs suddenly grew tout, attempted to pull her down, but she dug her nails into the diamond with vicious abandon.

Her hand was as hot as a forge and the diamond screamed in fury and agony. The metal breastplate had begun to melt, strands of molten silver sliding down Xellah's chest and she clutched the jewel, which was beating like a heart.

"What are you doing, you cannot…the diamond!" Master Teoath yelled, though he had no mouth and no tongue anymore, speaking with the fury of the waters and the clacking bones.

Now a tendril wrapped itself around Yalxi's neck. She held on to the jewel. It was no longer attached to the breastplate and it did not have the hardness of diamond. It had turned soft and slick and tried to wrestle itself away. She wrapped her hand around it, making a tight fist and she let it burn, hotter and hotter.

It glowed white inside her palm, light trickling out. Then it was a black inkiness as it became a lump of coal and this blackness burnt her eyes, as hot as an underwater sun. But still she wouldn't let go until it turned into a gray powder.

The tendrils dissolved, also turning into ash, and then even that ash was gone and she held nothing.

She felt lightheaded and her body was growing numb. Still, she grabbed Xellah by the arm and began pulling him with her. She swam up, the water almost painful against her skin. She could barely see when she reached the surface and managed to drag them both onto through a clump of reeds, until they were sprawled upon the shore of the lake.

She heard him cough and then there was darkness.

She rolled over and opened her eyes to a murky dawn. When she brushed a hand against her head she felt pain and saw the bandage. She sat up slowly and looked around. Yalxi lay under a tree. He was sitting farther away, standing under the open sky, as if searching for the rising sun.

He turned, as if he'd sensed her eyes on him.

"How do you feel?"

She said nothing, pressed her injured hand against her chest. She had blisters on her hand and a missing finger. He looked no better. There were raw, red bruises around his neck, like a man who has escaped the noose.

"Come now. I don't intend to hurt you."

She chuckled at that. But someone had bandaged her hand and she was still breathing, after all. He could have crushed her head with a rock while she lay sleeping and she would have never known it.

"I feel a little bit broken this morning."

"Yes. I can't say it's a very good morning."

"Depends who you ask, I suppose."

She glanced at the lake. The waters were ordinary now, the green film that had covered it had disappeared and all magic was truly gone from this place. They'd rid themselves of Teotah at long last.

"I did not think you'd ever do anything like that," Xellah said, as if guessing her thoughts.

"It's what we said we would do, once long ago. We would destroy the diamond."

"I know. Long ago."

She attempted to stand up. Her legs were wobbly and he stepped forward and gave her a hand. She let herself stand next to him for a moment, clasping his arm, before taking a breath and stepping back.

"I should have burnt it away years ago. But I wanted its power too much," she admitted.

"You didn't have to let me live."

She shook her head. "Itzyul would have been disappointed if I hadn't. And I already disappointed her so many times. Now I've finally made the correct choice."

"We both chose wrong."

They looked at each other. He had flecks of gray in his hair, his eyes were tired. How easily time and cruelty had worn them down. If Itzyul could see them perhaps they would be completely unrecognizable.

He bowed his head and clasped her uninjured hand, touching the pearl ring.

"I apologize most humbly and renounce my title. You are the Mistress of the Sorcerers' Guild."

"Oh, no," she said and almost laughed at that. "I should have never had that title."

Xellah looked at her quizzically and nodded. "Then I still apologize most humbly." He lowered his head. "I truly do, Yalxi and cannot begin to express my sorrow. I must repay you one day, for your mercy."

She slid her hand away from him. By the dead tree she found her bag of supplies and hefted it on her shoulders. Xellah looked at her with curiosity.

"What are you doing?" he asked.

"I'll be heading off now."

"To the city?"

"No, although you must return there. When you do, ensure my apprentices are safe and pursue no violence against the Guild of Thieves."

"I'll do as you say, though I won't be able to remain Master Sorcerer for long after this."

"I know," she said simply.

Her body was tense under his gaze. Not that she expected him to attack her, not now. It was only that she wasn't quite sure what he'd say.

"There are bandits on these roads, Yalxi. It's best if you don't travel alone," he told her.

"I'll keep an eye out for them."

"I'd accompany you if you'd ask."

"And maybe I would have said yes, once," she admitted and turned from him. "But you're not the boy I knew and I'm not the girl I was. Mercy is not forgiveness, and forgetting is no easy task even if I once managed to erase almost my entire past."

"Yet, my debt—"

"You owe no debt to me. But remember your debt to Itzyul. We promised we'd be just and lied. We must keep our word, now."

He touched her arm and she turned her head and looked at him. There was something of the boy she'd known in his face, after all, and she smiled at that boy and he smiled back. Then she was off, walking slowly.

Much later, when they had reached a little inn by the side of the room and had availed themselves to a room, the nahual became a snowy fox and sat at her feet, watching her with its bright eyes.

"Well, that was all very silly. You have no knife, little money and a lot of bruises now."

"Did you want me to keep the diamond?"

"Of course not. But he could have managed some sort of transport or reward for us, couldn't he?"

"I don't need a reward from him."

"I would have wanted a reward."

Yalxi lay back on the bed, pulling the threadbare covers up to her chin and feeling oddly comforted. When she'd been a girl she'd spent the night in many an inn likes this, trying to sleep in lumpy beds riddled with fleas while other apprentices snored. She hadn't missed any of it, but now she felt a certain twinge of recognition and the wide open roads could not frighten her. She'd been there before.

"How about *I* give you a reward?" she asked. "You've always been good to me and I haven't always been a kind mistress. Once we reach a town with a guild, I can ensure you have a new young master."

Yes, she recalled the days when the world held promises. And perhaps the nahual wished to regain some of that. Such things couldn't be found with Yalxi, her bones grown weary, her mutilated hand resting gently against her chest. But someone else might be able to provide it. Some eager, upstart sorcerer who would cradle the ring between her hands, treasure it with her life.

She looked at the white fox and the fox frowned. "That is not the way of sorcerers, to give power and secrets up."

"It is the way of friends, though."

The fox tilted its head. "Your blood must truly be thinning, Yalxi. But no. What would I do? Waste my days listening to some pimpled youth chatter on about spells and potions? Or even worse, if I were to find myself in the company of an incompetent, incontinent third-rate sorcerer who can hardly chew his food?"

"Incontinent!"

"It's rather common at a certain point."

"You do realize one day I may have trouble chewing my food?"

The fox jumped upon the bed and bumped its head against her arm. "You do realize that despite your numerous and well documented flaws I actually like you?"

"I like you too."

"And what you did…it was stupid and brave and just. And I'd rather stay by the side of an idiotic yet idealistic sorcerer than the most powerful, young mage in the world."

"Your blood must be thinning too for you to say that."

The fox grinned and pretended to bite her hand, but it was the play of a pup. She pulled its ear and ran her fingers through its fur. It was getting late and her eyes were heavy.

"Yalxi, you should rest," the nahual said. "For adventure surely awaits tomorrow and barring that there will be breakfast."

"You dreadful thing, always thinking with your stomach," she whispered and pressed her cheek against the fox's back, feeling its softness as the animal yawned.

The fox was warm against her belly. The world felt small and gentle. And for once in a very long time she slept soundly, a perfect dreamless sleep. For adventure could indeed wait until tomorrow and there were no great deeds to accomplish, nor towering ambitions to heed. Neither revenge, nor spite. There was just a serene, lovely moment and the chirping of crickets outside and the night all around them. It was the two of them, like in the beginning.

It was enough.